A MESSAGE FROM CHICKEN HOUSE

My cat Mabel bosses me around ... she'd fit right in with this bunch of feline friends! They're all different – but all determined to solve the mystery behind the new arrival. With lots of lovely pictures, this is a charming and funny ~~tail~~ tale for everyone who *knows* their pets have more to say! Plus, the author and illustrator have been friends forever – and so have their cats!

BARRY CUNNINGHAM
Publisher
Chicken House

Hotel FOR Cats

Marie Pavlenko & Marie Voyelle

Translated by Anna Brooke

Chicken House

2 Palmer Street, Frome, Somerset BA11 1DS

First published in France by Flammarion Jeunesse under the title
Charamba: Hôtel pour Chats. Text and illustrations © 2022 Éditions Flammarion, Paris

First published in Great Britain in 2024
Chicken House
2 Palmer Street
Frome, Somerset BA11 1DS
United Kingdom
www.chickenhousebooks.com

Chicken House/Scholastic Ireland, 89E Lagan Road, Dublin Industrial Estate,
Glasnevin, Dublin D11 HP5F, Republic of Ireland

Marie Pavlenko and Marie Voyelle have asserted their right under the Copyright,
Designs and Patents Act 1988 to be identified as the author and illustrator of this work.

English translation by Anna Brooke © Chicken House 2024

Cover illustration © Emily Fox 2024
Cover design by Steve Wells
Typeset by Dorchester Typesetting Group Ltd
Printed in Great Britain by Clays, Elcograf S.p.A

FSC
www.fsc.org
MIX
Paper | Supporting
responsible forestry
FSC® C018072

1 3 5 7 9 10 8 6 4 2

British Library Cataloguing in Publication data available.

ISBN 978-1-915947-00-0
eISBN 978-1-915947-11-6

To my cats, past and present: Tao, Anakin, Leïa, Sookie and Obiwan, not to mention Esmeralda and Gelsamina. And to Mathias and Aurélien, of course. – MARIE PAVLENKO

To Swing, Moune and Kida (thank you, Amandine P. and Gauthier B.). To my 'child-who-thinks-she's-a-cat', Saskia. To my mother who let me have a cat as a child :) To Maïck and Nelly, my grandmothers. And a special mention for Collo. – MARIE VOYELLE

SOME
CHARACTERS
IN THIS
STORY

MAGDA

A kindly French lady, about seventy-five years old, who loves flower-print dresses, milky tea and squashy cushions.

She's in charge of a rather unusual establishment in Paris, France: Hotel Charamba, a hotel for cats. It's a place where pet cats stay when their families go away on holiday (for a weekend, a week, a month . . .). Magda feeds them, cuddles them and sometimes spends hours throwing them mice (don't worry, not real mice – ones that she has knitted herself!).

Magda has also invented a brilliant cat-food distribution system, but more about that later.

So, you see, she's a lovely lady and is convinced that she's the head of the household.

BUT SHE'S WRONG.

THE REAL MASTERS OF THE HOUSE ARE:

BOBINE

(That's the French word for 'bobbin', or a 'spool of thread'. It's pronounced *Bob-een*.)

Bobine is an old female Persian cat with very long, tangled white hair. She has pawful trouble with her matted clumps of fur and dreads being brushed.

She once lost a fang in a fight with a bull-dog. The dog, by the way, still has the tooth lodged in its bottom.

She has grown calmer with age. Hates noise. Laps up nettle soup as if it were milk.

Distinctive feature: she secretly wants to learn how to knit (so sits for hours, still as a statue, watching Magda).

MULOT

(It's the French word for 'field mouse', pronounced *Mu-low*. Why would anyone call a cat *Mouse*?)

Mulot is a black-and-white moggy who Magda found abandoned in a bin when he was just two days old. He was curled up with a family of mice. Magda fed him with a bottle and saved his life.

Mulot hates his name. (Can you blame him? How would you like to be called after something you might eat, like Cheeseburger or Rice Krispies?)

He's a strong cat who loves to strut his stuff, show off his muscles and look for fights. But deep down he's a propurr softy.

Distinctive feature: an intense fear of cucumbers.

CARPETTE

(Pronounced as it reads, *Car-pette* is the French word for 'rug'.)

Carpette is a middle-aged Siamese male who thinks he was a human in a previous life. Carpette loves to sing to his fellow lodgers. He's also looking for love – he's convinced his soulmate must be out there, somewhere. (The question is, where?) He often speaks to his future love when he's alone (or *thinks* he is).

Distinctive feature: a fan of Elton John, he meows non-stop on the off-chance a record producer might be passing and hear him.

COUSCOUSSE

(Magda's funny spelling of 'couscous', pronounced *Coos-coos*.)

A chubby female Chartreux (her tummy drags on the floor), Couscousse was one of Magda's first ever lodgers, but her owners never came back to get her.

Couscousse lives in her own little dream world, inventing stories that she believes are true. For example, she thinks she can communicate with the ghost of Albert Einstein (or Berty, as she calls him). She asks him questions all the time.

Distinctive feature: she pretends to have studied at university in America.

BUT MAGDA KNOWS NONE OF THIS . . .

1. SUF-FUR-CATING HEAT

So, there you have it. You've met all the characters, and so now it's time for our story. Ready? Let's go.

It all started one late morning in July, when a man in a velvet suit stopped in front of the glass doors of the cat hotel.

It was a hot day. A scorching day, in fact. And so sunny that the neon-orange 'Charamba' sign, whose lights were usually so strong they could be seen from the far end of the street at night, seemed almost pale.

Not that the man noticed. He was hot and flustered and needed to mop his brow, which is why he put down the carrier he'd been holding, and drew a hankie from his pocket.

Which is when a yowl escaped from the carrier.

Inside, there was a dragon – a magnificent blue-scaled dragon who ate nothing but blackberries and apple tree leaves and . . . Nah! I'm joking! Dragons don't exist! Well, not in real life. Though they *do* exist in pretend life. But as this is real life and not pretend life, I can tell you it wasn't a dragon.

What it *was* was a cat. (Obviously – this book's full of them.) A black cat.

And although to the man the yowl had sounded like a 'meoooowww . . .', what the cat in the carrier had really said was, 'You got to be kitten me! I'm dying in here. Paw-lease hurry up!'

'Don't worry, Wolfgang, everything's going to be fine,' the man cooed in reply, walking through the hotel door without the slightest idea of what Wolfgang had said.

'I'm not worried, Norbert,' the cat squeaked. 'I'm just desperate for a weeeeeee!'

What can I say?

That's the problem with humans, isn't it? They think they're cleverer than other

creatures, but really, they don't understand very much – especially not cat-speak (or whale-speak or giraffe-speak, at that . . .). Cats understand humans though, which is clawesome!

The door opened into a large chintzy lobby, at the back of which sat a huge wooden desk, topped with a computer. To say the desk was cluttered would be an understatement. See for yourself.

Around the computer were: piles of folders, heaps of pens (pink, green and black), a figurine of a pig sipping cocktails, a purple wig, a stapler shaped like a pear, several plants (including a heart-shaped cactus), knitting needles, two or three balls of wool, three cat-themed mugs filled with dregs of tea and a big fan blowing air at full blast.

And in front of it all sat a white Persian cat

with very tangled fur, who didn't so much as bat a whisker when the man in the velvet suit walked over and called, 'Hellooooo?'

'Comiiiiiiing!' came the high-pitched reply, as an elderly lady in a yellow-and-mauve flowery dress burst through the door behind the desk. 'Ah, *bonjour*!' she said (which means 'hello' in French). The creases around her blue eyes wrinkled like piped buttercream as she smiled. 'I'm Magda. And you must be ...'

'Norbert,' said Norbert, holding out his hand. 'We spoke on the phone ... about Wolfgang's stay ... .for two weeks.'

'Oh, yes, yes!' Magda

peered into Wolfgang's carrier for a moment.

But Wolfgang thought he'd die of embarrassment!

You see, the pee that had needed to come out before, was coming out *now*, in the corner, like water gushing from a tap! *A cat-astro-pee!* Wolfgang thought. *I've never felt so embarrassed!*

'Ah, Wolfgang's busy,' said Magda sweetly. She stretched out her hand towards the white Persian. 'This is Bobine, our eldest. Say *bonjour*, Bobine!'

Bobine didn't move.

Magda turned to Norbert. 'Would you like to see Wolfgang's room? He's in number 13, and he'll be perfectly fine.'

'I'd love to,' said Norbert.

'Meooooowww!' said Wolfgang, which meant, 'Oh, the shame of it, Norbert! This is paw-sitively terrible. Peeing myself the second we arrive! Why didn't you go faster? I'll be the laughing stock of the hotel.' And he put his paws on either side of the carrier's walls, so as not to get them wet.

Then, still without the slightest idea of what Wolfgang had said, Norbert followed Magda through a door behind the desk, into a corridor covered in paintings of cats – kittens, pedigrees, alley cats, even cats wearing hats and scarves – and up a steep floral-carpeted staircase towards Room 13.

It was then that Bobine decided it was time to follow – to make sure, as any self-respecting hotel cat should always do, that their new boarder got settled in. So, she leapt off the desk in front of the fan, which blew her fur up into a funny punk hairstyle, and set off behind Magda, three times fluffier than before.

Now it's time for me to tell you something very important that is going to affect the rest of our story.

I'm going to stop translating cat-speak.

Up until now, when a cat has spoken, you've always read 'meoooowww', followed by the human translation. But, from this page onwards, I'm only going to write the words in human.

OK?

Good.

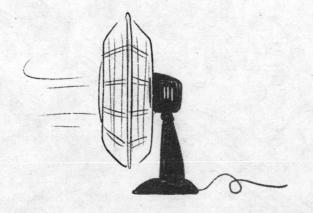

2. GOOD MEOW-NING!

Now, where were we?

Oh yes.

Twenty minutes later, Norbert had left Wolfgang and the cat hotel behind.

He was on his way to Naples in Italy and was about to drive there in his open-top car – wind in his hair – all the way through France, across the Alps (the mountains that separate France and Italy) and past the Italian capital of Rome. And it was going to be a

17

lovely trip (if you get the chance to do it one day, you should; it's a beautiful part of the world).

'Ah! *La dolce vita*!' he sighed contentedly (that means 'This is the life' in Italian – he was thinking of all the pizza and coffee-flavoured ice cream he was going to eat) as he disappeared around the corner, a spring in his step.

Inside the hotel, Wolfgang was hoping to do a bit of disappearing of his own. He was frantically searching his new room, looking for a place where no one would find him. He would have done anything – shave his fur, stand in the rain, swallow a furball – to avoid being seen …

As for Bobine, after walking Norbert to the front door with Magda, she had popped into the kitchen for a quick snack and was now on her way back up the stairs to Room 13 to see how the little newcomer was getting on.

'Knock-knock,' she said. 'Can I come in?'

'Eek!' Wolfgang dipped behind a squishy ball, but it was only three centimetres high, so, as you might guess, he was as visible as . . . well . . . a cat hiding behind a very small ball.

Bobine pushed her super-fluffy head through the cat flap. 'Hello!' she said kindly.

'N-n-no-one's here! Empty room!' squeaked Wolfgang, wishing he could transform himself into something else – a banana, maybe . . . or a sausage. No, not a sausage (cats eat those). An umbrella, perhaps?

Bobine looked at him thoughtfully for a second, then walked through the cat flap (which, I'm pleased to say, flattened her coat and returned it to normal).

Wolfgang panicked and backed away.

Bobine rolled her eyes.

'Calm down. I'm not going to hurt you. I'm an O.A.P.!'

'A-a-an O.A-what?' Wolfgang stuttered.

'O.A.P. Old Aged Puss! The oldest cat in the hotel, actually. I don't even hurt flies.'

And to prove it, she opened her mouth wide.

Wolfgang hissed. Usually when cats show their teeth, it means 'Let's have a fight!'

'No, no, no. Look at my fangs. "Ees ones 'ere,' said Bobine coolly, her mouth open wide again. 'An' 'urry up. M' jaw's achin'!'

Suddenly curious, as all cats are when faced

with something unexpected, Wolfgang flattened his body like a rug and, despite himself, shuffled over for a closer look, his ears pointing upwards like arrows.

'Can 'oo see 'em?' asked Bobine.

'The yellow ones?' he said.

Bobine threw him a look that said, 'Yellow? You cheeky mog!'

Wolfgang looked again.

'Oo-oh, your fangs! You . . . y-you've only got one!'

'Bingo!'

'What happened?'

Bobine closed her mouth and sat down. Wolfgang sat down too – but at a safe distance.

'Well, a long time ago,' she started, 'I lived in the countryside, next door to a tabby cat called Brutus. He was a big cat. But he wasn't big enough to fight off a bulldog. So, I decided to help.'

'You fought a dog to help your neighbour?'

'Course I did. I like taking care of other cats. That's my thing. I sunk my fang into that bully of a dog's behind good and *pro-purr* . . . and it's been there ever since!'

For the first time since his arrival, Wolfgang smiled. But it was short-lived. Because seconds later, another head poked through the cat flap. The head of an enormous cat with grey fur and long, thick whiskers that looked like walrus tusks.

'Good meow-ning!' said the walrus.

Wolfgang jumped straight back down behind the squishy ball.

'Ah, come on in, Couscousse,' said Bobine. 'Meet our newbie.'

Now, this might be a good time to take a little break. So go make yourself a drink, nip to the loo, or eat a biscuit or something and I'll meet you back here in, oh, about three minutes and twenty seconds. OK?

You see, Couscousse was huge, and the cat flap was tiny, so it was like trying to squeeze a football into a bottle!

But Couscousse was flexible, despite her size, and above all else, very determined, so she pushed and squirmed and wiggled and thrust, and eventually (I'd say after four minutes twenty-one seconds, actually) she entered the room with an 'OOF!'

'*¡Hola!*' she said happily, licking her sides with catisfaction.

'O . . . ola?' Wolfgang repeated, completely confused.

'This is Wolfgang. Wolfgang, meet Cous-cousse,' said Bobine. 'She lives here full-time, like me. And as you can see, she can speak Spanish!'

'You all have very funny names,' observed Wolfgang.

'What? What's funny about Bobine and Couscousse?' said Bobine. 'They're purr-fectly nice names! There's Carpette and Mulot too.'

'Mulot! You live with a field mouse?'

'No, Mulot's a cat. A big one. His room's three doors down.'

'A cat called Field Mouse?'

'Yes.'

'S-s-so if Field Mouse is a cat, what do you call the mice?' Wolfgang smiled.

But Bobine threw him another one of her looks – which was a shame, because Wolfgang had been attempting a joke, which in my opinion is the best way to break the ice. But unfortunately for Wolfgang, the one thing cats weren't allowed to do in Hotel Charamba was poke fun at Mulot's name – but, of course, Wolfgang couldn't have known that.

'Yes . . . Sorry . . . Of course. Field Mouse. Great name for a cat. Makes paw-fect sense,' he mewed nervously, before adding, 'A-and who's Carpette?'

'Our fourth full-time resident,' said Bobine. 'He's showing a couple of other newbies around the cat common room, or as we call it, "the Pawesome Palace"! The hotel fills up fast in summer, so there's always loads of us in there.'

At that exact moment, a loud meowing sound came from the main hallway, causing Wolfgang to panic and dash behind his litter tray.

'Don't you want to come to the Pawesome Palace?' said Couscousse. 'It's got cool, rectangular thingies!' (Couscousse's name for the climbing boxes in the room.)

Wolfgang quaked.

'N-n-n-n . . . no thanks!' he managed to squeal.

'OK. You get yourself settled in, then,' said Bobine gently. 'Then, when you're ready, give us a "mew" and we'll go together. The Pawesome Palace is full of games, scratchy trees, perchy spots, secret passages, tubes, ladders, strings, rectangular thingies of course, and really nice cats.

'It's the most clawesome place in the hotel! You'll see. And you're here for two weeks, so you may as well make some friends. Come on,

Couscousse . . . See you later, Wolfgang!'

Wolfgang didn't answer, so the two cats leapt back through the flap.

Well, Bobine leapt. Couscousse pushed and squirmed and wiggled and thrust for at least three minutes and twenty-seven seconds this time, until she finally squeezed through with a big POP!

CLING!

3. THINKING CAT ON

Remember I told you that Magda had invented an automatic cat-food distribution system?

Well, I'm going to tell you about it now, before we go any further, because it was such a brilliant system, I've been desperate to describe it and I can't wait any more.

It was a transparent tube that delivered the cats' food straight into their rooms. It started in the kitchen on the ground floor (where

31

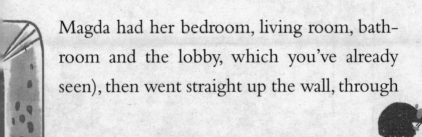

Magda had her bedroom, living room, bath-room and the lobby, which you've already seen), then went straight up the wall, through the ceiling and into the corridor on the first floor, where it ran along the ceiling to fork off into each room, stopping a few centimetres above each bowl.

The way it worked was this: Magda poured the food into the tube in the kitchen, pressed a button, then –VROOM! – it whooshed along the pipe before landing in the cats' bowls with a delicious 'crispycrunchytumbly' noise. (Sorry, I know, 'crispycrunchytumbly' isn't a word, but I wrote it and I like it, so it's staying.)

And if the cats got hungry outside mealtimes, all they had to do was place their feet on a little paw-shaped mat and – *crispycrunchytumble!* –

the food would fill their bowls in under ten seconds *flat*.

It even had a clever sensor that stopped mischievous moggies from popping their paws on the mat non-stop: when the bowls were full, the sensor knew it and no more food would come out.

The whole invention was Magda's, but she'd had a little help from her friend Margaret, who was very good at taking measurements for the machinery. (Because sometimes two brains are better than one. It's called teamwork. Remember that, if

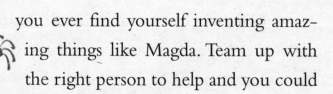

you ever find yourself inventing amazing things like Magda. Team up with the right person to help and you could go a long way!) Both Magda and Margaret were very proud of their invention.

And for good reason. The machine was great.

Now, Magda noticed that Wolfgang hadn't come out of his room on the first day.

Or on the second day.

Or even on the third day.

But she respected all her boarders' personalities and put it down to shyness.

'Don't worry, sweetheart,' she said, stroking him every morning and evening, as he rubbed himself against her leg with a 'mew!'. 'Your friend Norbert will be back soon.'

But Bobine and Couscousse weren't so sure.

They'd tried everything they could to re-assure Wolfgang, but he just stayed in his room and hid whenever anyone poked their noses through the flap.

Bobine took this particularly to heart: over the years, she'd managed to make every cat feel at home at Charamba. The hotel was a place for all cats, of all ages, all types of fur and all personalities. Even the shy ones loved it.

But Wolfgang?

What on earth was wrong with him?

She'd tried winning him over with ball-rolling, gambolling, invitations to post-scratching, fast-running (also known as 'the zoomies' – you know, when cats run wildly around a room with their eyes wide) and feather-dangling – even when the string had got caught in her long white hair.

But nothing had worked.

Wolfgang was still a little ball of worry.

Which was very disturbing.

What on earth were she and Couscousse going to do? The reputation of the hotel was on the line!

And that's when it hit her:

Couscousse!

Could Couscousse be the problem? She had, after all, insisted on introducing Wolfgang to Albert Einstein's ghost . . .

Couscousse had even given Wolfgang the whole Einstein backstory, telling him, as she did anyone who would listen (and even those who wouldn't) that her love of maths had started when she'd bumped into him at university in America, where they'd been drawn together like magnets.

He could understand cat-speak, she'd said, and they got on so well together they could chat about equations and maths theories and formulas and rectangular thingies all day long.

Berty wasn't real, of course. Couscousse just had a wild imagination.

But could this be the cause of Wolfgang's discomfort? Wolfgang's whiskers had tightened

with terror at the mention of Berty's name. And things had only got worse since.

That must be it!

There wasn't a meow-ment to lose. Wolfgang might get sick if things carried on like this.

Bobine had to do something, and she'd start, she thought, by asking Couscousse to stop visiting him.

'I know Berty's important to you,' she said carefully, a little later that day, 'but I don't think Wolfgang's ready to hear about a ghost. I think he's too young.'

'What do you mean?' said Couscousse, taken aback. 'Berty's a-meow-zing! He knows everything about everything!'

'I know,' said Bobine, gently. 'He's fantastic. But think of Wolfgang . . .'

And Couscousse trusted Bobine, so she accepted.

Bobine decided it was time to bring in a

new cat: Carpette was a showman through and through. *Maybe he could help?*

So, on the fourth morning, Carpette and Bobine stepped through the flap into Wolf-gang's room.

Wolfgang tried to hide but his fur was black and his scratchy tree was beige, so he stood out like, erm . . . well . . . a black cat on a beige scratchy tree.

In fact, he looked so silly that Bobine would have liked to laugh. But she didn't. She was too worried. Plus, there was a puddle of wee in the middle of the room, which was not a good sign.

'Erm . . . h–had a little accident in the night?' Carpette stammered uneasily.

You see, cats are very clean animals. And Wolfgang was young and healthy, so there was no reason for him to have peed outside his litter tray.

Wolfgang let out a strangled, 'Sorry!'

'Forget about it,' said Bobine quickly. 'I'll get Magda to clean it up. Right now, there's some-one I want you to meet. Wolfgang, this is Carpette.'

Carpette moved over to greet Wolfgang with a wag of his tail, as Siamese cats do.

'I'm a musician in a band,' he mewed, widening his dazzling blue eyes. 'Not a bad one, either, if I do say so myself.' Wolfgang eyed him from his tree.

'Would you like a private concert?' Carpette

offered. 'I'm great at Elton John songs.'

'N-no thank you!'

Carpette couldn't believe his pointy ears!
What sort of cat didn't want to hear his pawesome, purr-fectly rhythmical voice?

'You don't like Elton John?' he spluttered.
'He's famous all over the world! Even in the
North Pole! If they could hear him on Mars,
the Martians would be smitten as kittens too!'

Carpette noticed that the more he spoke,
the more Wolfgang curled up into a little ball.

Hmmm … he was going to have to try something else.

'Did you know that I used to be a human?' Carpette said, very matter-of-cat … erm … matter-of-factly.

Bobine immediately nudged Carpette in the chest.

'What d'you do that for? It's true! I used to play the drums, the electric guitar and the trombone and everything. My fans loved me. Ladies would swoon. I wore flared trousers and dark sunglasses, even at night. Once, even …'

'Carpette!' Bobine hissed.

'What?'

'You know what!'

Earlier, Bobine had warned Carpette about talking about his previous life as a human. 'We're dealing with a shy and frightened cat here,' she'd said. 'We need him to relax. So you can sing and dance, but purr-lease don't mention your "specialness". You can tell him all about your human life when he's feeling better, OK?'

'OK!' Carpette had promised. Yet here he was blurting out everything.

Bobine's ears drooped in despair.

And Wolfgang looked terrified.

But Carpette, unaware, carried on.

'Reincarnation isn't all it's cracked up to be, you know. It's really hard to play guitar and trombone when you're a cat. But I was lucky.' He puffed out his chest. 'I could have come back as a hot-air balloon, and then I wouldn't have been able to hold an instrument at all.'

'Erm, Carpette,' said Bobine, rolling her eyes. 'You couldn't have come back as a hot-air balloon because they're not alive! They're vehicles. Like bikes and trains.'

'No, they're not!' Carpette hissed, suddenly looking cross. 'Hot-air balloons are living, loving souls! Humans just want us to think they are objects so they can exploit them. Well, I won't let them. One day, I shall free them all!'

And with that, he turned about sharply and leapt out through the cat flap.

Bobine studied Wolfgang for a long time after that, watching as the little cat tried to avoid her stare.

Then she sat down and stretched out her back leg to *paws* for thought . . . sorry, I meant nibble on her paw *as she thought*.

Then she stopped thinking and nibbling and decided that the best thing to do was just ask:

'Why don't you want to come to the Pawesome Palace?'

'I don't like other cats!' Wolfgang spluttered.

'But I saw you the other day through the flap,' said Bobine. 'I tiptoed over. You were chasing a ball and rolling around – until you heard a noise, which made you jump up on to the tree. You were happy one minute, then . . . I don't know.

I'm sure you do like cats.'

'I don't.'

'But you haven't even tried to come to the Pawesome Palace. If you're scared, I can stay right by you.'

'No thanks. I'm purr-fectly fine on my own.'

'But the Palace is a very friendly place. Everyone loves it. It's full of rectangular thing-ies!' said Bobine, running out of arguments.

But Wolfgang just turned and lay down, showing his bum.

So Bobine left with a sigh.

She'd rarely felt so perplexed.

Her instinct (which was never wrong) told her Wolfgang was hiding something.

It also told her that neither Couscousse nor Carpette were to blame.

So what was the problem?

And this thing about not liking cats? Bobine didn't believe it for a second.

Hmmmm! There was only one thing for it: she was going to have to get her thinking cat – sorry, cap – on.

4. SHAKESPURR!

That night, Bobine called an Emergency Meeting in the Pawesome Palace.

She'd seen one on TV once, with humans who'd got together in an official-looking place to talk about important things and make important decisions. (Though none of the humans in the show had actually done what they'd said they'd do once they got home. Bobine – as the most senior and reliable cat in Charamba – had every intention of implementing whatever

49

ideas the cats came up with. 'For Wolfgang! For the hotel's reputation!')

And so, at half past midnight, four shadows sneaked into the empty Pawesome Palace.

Sorry, did I say four? I meant three.

The fourth one had to wiggle and push and jiggle and squeeze and didn't get in until at least thirty-five minutes past twelve.

But once they were all together, they were a fine, solemn, superbly whiskered-looking crew. Like the Four Mus-cat-eers!

There was Bobine, of course, Couscousse, Carpette and Mulot, who looked like a 1930s film star, with his big strong muscles and debonair black and white markings (he had a chic black 'mask' over half of his head).

Bobine licked her feet as she waited for the others to settle in. Then once each cat had parked their paws on a rectangular thingy, she began.

'I have brought you here today to talk about something very serious.'

'Erm. I have a question!' Couscousse interrupted. 'Can Berty join in?'

Bobine sighed and said yes.

'Really? So, I can tell you what he's saying?'

Everybody sighed and said yes.

'Good! So . . . well, Berty

a sourpuss, he's just scared.'

'I agree,' said Bobine.

Couscousse's tail twitched

ment.

'But what's he scared of?'

'Erm . . .' Couscousse's ta.

doesn't know!'

'OK, not to worry. Thank

I mean Albert. Now on to tʰ

What I had wanted to say wa.

take Wolfgang to the Paweso

stay with him, but he said "nʊ

'And he didn't want to listeⁿ

either,' complained Carpette.

him a private concert! I mean

'Mulot,' said Bobine, turnɪ.

hulk of a cat beside her, 'I dⁱ

help because you're so big anʊ

thought he'd faint at the sight

Mulot flexed his muscles wɪ.

You'll notice that Bobine didn't mention Wolfgang's little joke about Mulot's 'field mouse' name. If she'd done that, Wolfgang wouldn't have stood a chance. You see, like most cats, Mulot could be very sensitive.

If you've ever seen a cat trying to jump on a sideboard, or a shelf, but miss and fall, you'll know what I mean. Cats never just laugh off their failings. Oh no! They always walk away haughtily with a look that says, 'Me, miss a jump? Purr-lease! I wasn't even trying to jump.' And Mulot was just like every other cat, except ten times tetchier because of his name.

'Now, I don't mind if a quiet cat decides to stay in his or her room,' Bobine continued, 'but Wolfgang isn't a quiet one. He's playful and, I'm pretty sure, sociable.' She paused, thoughtfully. 'Something is blocking him and I don't like it. Our mission in Hotel Charamba is to make every cat feel at home, so we need to get to the bottom of this. Friends, I need your help. I need your ideas.'

'I say we put on a concert,' suggested Carpette.

'No. No,' said Couscousse, 'how about we stop feeding him, then leave a trail of cat food between his room and the Pawesome Palace? He'll be so hungry he'll have to go!'

'Nah. Nah. I know,' said Carpette excitedly. 'We get dressed up as plants, then kidnap him and throw him into the Palace!'

'Carpette!'

'What? Plants are harmless. He'd understand!'

'Or,' Couscousse continued, 'we could talk to him for hours, until he gets so fed up he leaves the room of his own accord.'

Bobine thought Couscousse might be on to something with that one – but only for a second. Because no, they had to help Wolfgang by being nice, not by being annoying.

And so – *to and fro, to and fro* – the cats knocked around all sorts of ideas like fluffy mice on string, but they couldn't agree on anything, until . . .

'I quite liked Carpette's idea,' said Mulot eventually.

'My plant-disguise-kidnapping one?' said Carpette enthusiastically.

'No. The first one. The performing one,' Mulot replied in his deep gravelly voice.

Then he slowly licked his paw and wiped his left eye, twice. The others waited for him to finish washing. 'Sorry! Speck of dust,' he mewed, before adding, 'Confidence . . . We want him to trust us, don't we?'

Bobine nodded.

'So, it's simple. Cats trust other cats who make them laugh. So, all we have to do is go into his room and put on a funny show. Nothing too fancy. Just a few simple acts. If we make him smile, he'll soon forget his problems and be jumping off those rectangular thingies in the Palace with us before you can say, "I'm feline fine!".'

'Could I sing for him?' said Carpette, quickly, his eyes shining brightly.

There was a short hesitation, then . . .

'Why not!' said Bobine.

'Yowlzers! Great. Wahoo! Mulot's plan it is!'

'What about you, Couscousse?'

'I could do a number with Berty . . .'

Bobine shuddered. 'Is that

really a good idea?'

'A brilliant one,' said Mulot. 'I'll think about what I can do too. I'm sure I can come up with something.'

'So that's settled then,' concluded Bobine. 'Emergency Meeting over.'

With the meeting finished, the cats all had a good stretch. Mulot flexed his front legs and pushed his bum into the air, while Carpette whooshed up a scratchy tree humming 'Rocket Man' (by Elton John, of course).

'What about our other boarders?' said Bobine, rubbing her cheeks on a chair leg. 'How's everyone else doing?'

A purring sound filled the Pawesome Palace.

'Prune, the elderly cat, still has arthritis

and the temper of a Dobermann,' said Mulot. 'But nothing I can't handle.'

'The three young 'uns who arrived the same day as Wolfgang are great,' said Couscousse. 'They love listening to Berty, they're brilliant at football and they already know every part of the hotel! It couldn't be better.'

'What are their names, again?'

'Speed and Hermann are the Siamese brothers. The ginger one's Grievous. I like him best. He knows Berty's theory of relativity!'

'So far so good then,' said Bobine.

'And Esmeralda's happy too,' said Carpette. 'Speed, Hermann and Grievous keep fighting for her attention, which she finds amusing. And she gets on well with old Prune.'

'There's Siegfried and

Constance too,' said Couscousse, making little mouse shapes on a scratchy mat with her claws. 'The Bengal cats who arrived on Thursday.

'They're a bit snobby, but we've seen worse. They stay in their room a lot. Constance asked if that was OK, and I said "yes", 'cause they both seem happy.'

'Purr-fect. The only problem we have then is Wolfgang,' said Bobine, trying to catch her own tail, before sitting down with a wild glint in her eye. 'So, I say we start preparing the show right away. Try and think of something fun and easy to perform. Nothing too complicated – No Shakespurr, OK? Then, we'll all meet in Room 13 at nine o'clock tomorrow morning. Got it?'

'Got it! . . . So long as there aren't any cucumbers,' added Mulot, the hair on his back suddenly standing on end.

'Not a single cucumber in sight. Promise,' said Bobine, reassuringly.

I think it's time I explained this whole cucumber thing.

Have you ever seen one of those horrible videos in which a human creeps up on a poor, unsuspecting cat (usually while they're eating their dinner) and places a cucumber on the floor behind them? When the cat sees the cucumber, it jumps at least three metres into the air and runs away, terrified.

Well, Magda's great-nephew did this once to Mulot — except he left cucumbers all over the hotel.

It was like walking through a cucumber-themed horror movie for Mulot. And today, because of this, he suffers from a bad case of cucumbaphobia (which isn't really a word but should be). It means he can't even think of a cucumber without the hackles on his back coming up.

But I'm getting distracted again, so let's get back to our friends.

5. CAT-ASTROPHE

At nine o'clock the next day, Bobine couldn't get into Room 13. There was a big hairy bum in the way! Couscousse's bum!

So she had to wait for . . .

One minute?

No.

Two?

No.

Three?

At least.

And when she finally got inside, she found Carpette and Mulot already there, preparing for the show, beneath a ball of black fur on a scratchy tree (Wolfgang, in case you hadn't guessed). And all around the room was the most terrible stench of pee-pee. URGH!

'Someone needs to have words with Magda!' said Mulot angrily. 'No boarder should have to put up with this!'

'You're right. Sorry, Wolfgang, Magda should have paid more attention to you,' said Bobine.

'It's nothing, I'm used to it . . .' Wolfgang sighed, his whiskers drooping.

'What do you mean, *used to it*?' said Bobine.

'Nothing. Forget it.'

But before Bobine could say 'Forget what?' Carpette had leapt into action.

'Enough of the chitter-catter! . . . Wolfgang,

boarder of Room 13, are you ready for the greatest show of your nine lives?'

'Sorry?'

'Hold on to your cat hat, because it's' – and he made a little drum roll sound with his paws on the floor – 'time for the BEST SHOW ON EARTH!'

Oh no, Carpette's getting carried away again, thought Bobine, but before she could stop him, he'd leapt on to a shelf with a stick in his jaws and – *uh-oh!* – knocked off a pot of catnip, which smashed onto the floor into a thousand pieces.

Not that that stopped him!

'I'm still standing, better than I ever did! Meow yeah!' he sang, as if nothing had happened.

(The words were mostly from the Elton John song, but with a few tweaks.)

'Looking like a true survivor, feeling like a catty kid.'

And as he sang, he stood up on his back legs.

And it was at that moment that something terrible happened:

You see, Carpette was convinced he had the most beautiful voice in the whole of catdom – a great, deep yowl like a human opera singer. But really, he caterwauled like a screeching train. (Or like a cat who'd had his paw cut off!)

Bobine and the others loved Carpette for his outgoing personality, his talk of romance and for his many other qualities – he had so many, in fact, that they'd almost forgotten he couldn't sing. (That's what friends do – they forgive your flaws.)

But Wolfgang didn't know Carpette very well, so he watched wide-eyed with terror, his fur standing on end and his ears twitching in all directions to escape the horrid sound.

But that wasn't the terrible part.

The terrible part was this:

Carpette, who over the years had seen far too many old-fashioned variety shows on TV, thought singers could only perform while standing on two legs, gripping a microphone.

But he didn't have a microphone; he had a stick.

And he didn't have two human legs, he had four cat ones (obviously). And a cat's back legs aren't designed to be stood up on, like human legs.

So after just three seconds of wild, upright cat wailing, the stick slipped and Carpette sprang to save it, but wobbled off-balance and accidentally kicked the stick through the air and – BAM! – straight into Wolfgang!

'Me-OW-OW-OW!' cried Wolfgang!

'AARGH!' cried Bobine, horrified. 'Quick, Mulot! Get Carpette down from that shelf!'

Couscousse took this as her cue to begin. And it was at that moment that everyone saw what she had been doing during Carpette's performance.

She'd been placing pellets from Wolfgang's litter tray in a rectangle shape on the floor.

'Dearest Wolfgang!' she began, with a big, pointy-fanged smile. 'From the heights of your scratchy tree, you can see that I have created here a board.'

Wolfgang (still recovering from his encounter with Carpette's stick) suddenly sat up and saw – to his horror – a disgusting clump of litter pellets with a space in the middle.

'And so, prepare to be wowed as I, Couscousse the Magni-fur-cent, demonstrate the theory of relativity – the very same theory (about space, time and gravity) developed by my dear friend Berty . . . the one and only Albert Einstein!'

She suddenly grabbed a piece of chalk

she'd hidden in a corner of the room and popped it into her mouth to 'write' on her 'board'.

'Imashine ish letter E here ish energy . . .'

She began tracing shapes (that no one understood) with the chalk, and as she did, her mouth (which was holding the chalk) started to drool.

'. . . and letsh shay ziz M here equalsh a mountain . . .'

Wolfgang studied Couscousse's movements, but he couldn't make head or tail of what he was supposed to be looking at. Was it meant to be funny or just plain revolting?

And then suddenly Couscousse froze – with her neck stretched out and her eyes and mouth wide open. Then her body jolted, and . . .

'Noooo!' cried Bobine.

But it was too late. (Sorry, this next bit's gross.) Couscousse threw up: *'BLURRRRR!'*

All over the floor!

Everyone looked on, stunned.

Couscousse tried to cover her puddle of chalky sick with some of the litter-tray pellets. Then, ears a-drooping, she headed to the cat flap muttering:

'Sorry. Furball . . . erm . . . chalk ball, actually. Probably shouldn't have put it in my . . . um . . . mouth. Bye!'

They needed to move on. Fast. And Mulot knew just what to do.

'Ladies and gentlecats, come closer if you

dare, for the time has come for some acro-cat-ics!'

Immediately, he began an amazing set of pirouettes, jumps, rolls and backflips. Honestly, they were so good, it was as if he'd been in a circus all his life.

And Wolfgang instantly sat up to watch with unexpected interest.

'Yessss!' Bobine dared to whis-purr to herself. 'We've done it!'

But she'd whis-purred too soon. Because remember the pot of catnip Carpette had broken earlier? Well, Mulot had suddenly slipped on it (after a particularly difficult backflip) and lost control. And he was now hurtling towards Wolfgang's scratchy tree – which he hit! – BOING, 'MRREOOW!' – causing Wolfgang to catapult across the room!

Don't worry, Wolfgang was OK. He'd landed upright (like most cats do) with his claws digging into the floor. But he'd had enough.

'Can you all leave, now. Please!'

Bobine didn't need asking twice. The whole show had been such a cat-astrophe, she didn't even wait for the others.

6. KNITTING KITTY

B obine spent the rest of the day curled in a ball in the corner of the sofa.

Actually, Bobine spent the rest of the day curled in a ball in the corner of the sofa *under* a pile of cushions, making sure nothing stuck out: not an ear, not a paw, not her tail. She didn't want to talk to anyone – not even to Couscousse, who came looking for her later that afternoon.

She wasn't being grumpy. She was just

feeling sad.

This had to be one of the worst days of her life!

Poor Wolfgang . . . he'd looked so unhappy. What on earth were they supposed to do now?

That night, Bobine didn't eat. She went straight to Magda (who was sitting in the ground-floor lounge) to tell her there was a problem – a problem big enough to ruin Charamba's entire reputation.

Purr-purr! Rub-rub! (The 'Rub-rub' part was Bobine's paws on Magda's legs as she tried

to get her attention.) But Magda was on the phone to Margaret, talking about a new motor for the food machine, and didn't pay her any attention.

'Meow-meow!' Rub-rub.

Bobine nudged against Magda's legs even harder and even made little figure-of-eight patterns on them with her paws. But Magda just stroked Bobine's head and chuckled to Margaret: 'What do you mean, "Germany"? I can't go that far . . . even to find the world's best motor. You know I couldn't leave my cats!' At which point, Bobine purred even more loudly (louder than any cat-food machine motor!) to make sure that Magda knew she was grateful for that last comment.

'What's going on, Bobine?' said Magda finally, as she put down the phone.

'Oh, it's terrible!' Bobine began, jumping on to Magda's lap. 'It's Wolfgang . . . I don't know what to do!' And she told her everything.

'But I've already filled your food bowl, sweetheart!' Magda cooed.

Bobine almost drew out her claws; she had to make Magda understand!

'And how are our guests doing? . . . The Bengal cats?' Magda continued. 'What are they called, again? Siegfried and Constance? They're used to being spoilt, aren't they, but they're eating, so they must be OK. I've knitted them a spider. I hope they'll like it.'

'Not the Bengals, Magda! Or any of the others. They're all fine!' Bobine closed her eyes and concentrated hard . . . 'Wolfgang!'

'Then there's that little black cat . . . Wolfgang!' Magda said, suddenly.

Bingo!

'He's very cute, but not toilet-trained – which is strange!'

But before Bobine could say anything else, Magda had pulled out her knitting box from under the sofa. And it was piled – *uh-oh!* – with lovely red and blue wool.

The effect on Bobine was immediate – as if someone had flicked a switch in her head.

So, as Magda picked up her knitting where she'd left off, Bobine lay down, helpless, pressing into Magda's tummy to watch the needles so intently that even an elephant-sized mouse in a tutu couldn't have distracted her.

Oh, how she wanted to learn to knit! 'The right-hand needle goes through the loop, then back on itself,' she purred. 'Then the loop goes under it . . . No, wait a moment . . . over it? Oh no. Meowzers. I'm lost!' And in her trance, all thoughts of poor little Wolfgang were suddenly forgotten.

The next morning, Bobine was fast asleep on Magda's sofa (though not under any cushions this time) when Mulot came charging over.

'Bobiiiiiiine!'

'MRREOW!' Bobine nearly hit the ceiling. 'Who? What?'

'Wolfgang's gone!'

'Pardon?'

'The little black cat . . .'

'Yes, I know who Wolfgang is!'

They dashed towards the stairs.

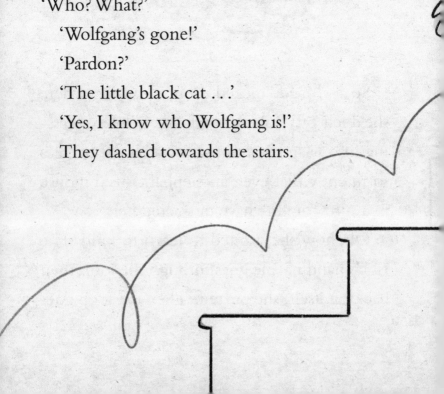

'No one's seen him today!' meowed Mulot.
'He's just disappeared!'

Bobine took the stairs to the first floor two
at a time!

7. HUNT THE CAT

When Bobine arrived in Wolfgang's room, Carpette and Couscousse were already there, sniffing around.

'I never realized just how much this room smelt of fear,' whispered Couscousse, her pupils wide with worry. 'We knew he was a nervous cat, but this . . .'

'Exactly,' said Mulot. 'We always noticed the . . . er . . . embarrassing smells, but really, this place reeks of more than that.'

'I've looked under every box, on every shelf and in every plaything,' confirmed Carpette. 'And he's not here.'

The four cats dashed to the Pawesome Palace, where the Siamese brothers, Speed and Hermann, were playing with Grievous, the ginger cat.

And what fun they were having: a ball pass here, a somersault there, a play claw fight in every corner. The room was crackling with their excitement!

Bobine and her friends dodged them, climbing ladders, checking hidey-holes, walking the shelves and leaping on to old armchairs and rectangular thingies. They moved cushions, litter trays and baskets and looked behind plant pots. Carpette visited every single scratchy pole and tree, but ...

NOTHING!

'You haven't seen Wolfgang, have you?' said Couscousse anxiously. 'Little black cat ... Shy?'

The three playmates carried on with their ball passes and noisy play-fights. Bobine had to duck to avoid being knocked out by Grievous's pass.

Suddenly, Mulot stopped the ball with his paw. 'Gentlecats,' he mewed loudly. 'We have asked you a question!'

'Meowzers! Sorry, we didn't hear,' said Speed, panting.

'What did you say?' said Hermann.

'Have you seen Wolfgang?'

Grievous gave a funny chuckle.

'Oh no. We haven't seen him, have we boys?' mewed Speed. 'No black cat around here.'

'Purr-cisely!' said Hermann. 'Thank goodness. They're bad luck!'

Bobine's eyes flashed with disbelief. How could they say such a thing? But before she could reply, a scream sounded.

It was coming from the room of the Bengal cats, Siegfried and Constance.

8. UNFURTUNATE COVER-UP

Bobine, as the most senior cat, threw herself through the cat flap first and landed nose-to-nose with Constance.

'Finally, madame. Could you please explain this awful situation?' Constance complained with a flick of her whiskers.

'W-what situation?' said Bobine, her eyes blinking.

'The menace-in-our-food-pipe situation. Never in all our nine lives have we seen anything like it!' complained Siegfried, whose black markings trembled with annoyance.

Bobine, Mulot, Carpette and Couscousse's head (the rest of her was still in the corridor) turned to look.

They couldn't believe their eyes!

There, wedged in Magda's food pipe at the end of the room, was something black, with four paws and a very squashed face.

'Wolfgang!'

Every centimetre of the little cat's body was stuck, except for a bit of ear, poking out the end.

Bobine rushed over with a yowl of despair. Wolfgang looked lifeless!

Mulot was quicker, leaping straight over Siegfried to stick his nose against the pipe. 'It's OK, he's breathing!' He sighed with relief. 'Wolfgang, buddy. Hold on in there. We're going to get you out!'

Bobine and Mulot pushed their paws inside

the pipe and slowly, gently, slid his little body out of the tight hole.

'It's all right,' reassured Bobine as Wolfgang flopped on to the floor. And to show him it was true, she began licking his tangled fur.

The others huddled around Wolfgang too, gently rubbing their heads on his body. Couscousse (who'd finally got through the flap) and Carpette made a barrier around him with their bodies and tails.

And for the first time in what felt like forever, Wolfgang knew that he was safe.

Suddenly, Siegfried and Constance gave a little cough (as some cats do).

'Could we have breakfast in peace now, purr-lease?' said Siegfried.

Mulot nudged Wolfgang to help him up, then, escorted by Carpette, Bobine and Couscousse, they left the room.

'Enjoy your meal, sir, madam,' said Couscousse as she tried to squeeze herself out.

'Sorry for the interruption. Won't happen again.'

Back in Room 13, Wolfgang immediately started telling the full story.

Can you guess what he said?

He said that some superstitious cats are scared of black cats because – and this is pawsitively ridiculous – they think they bring bad luck. And that all this nonsense had started almost as soon as Wolfgang had arrived, on the very first day. And that . . .

Hang on. Why don't I let *him* tell you in his own words?

'Speed and Hermann came to visit as soon as Magda and Norbert left,' he said. 'As soon as they saw me they hissed, then they roughed me up a bit with their claws and heads. They said if I left my room, I'd be in trouble. Grievous turned up later and did the same. And from then on, they kept coming back together.'

'Which is why there were puddles,' mumbled Couscousse.

'I'm so sorry!' Wolfgang hung his head. 'I was so scared. I never knew when they were going to turn up! And I'm not good at fighting . . .'

'And we couldn't even see what was going on right under our noses!' Carpette felt sickened and embarrassed. All cats have an excellent sense of smell. But the scent of Wolfgang's fear was so strong, it had filled the entire room, making it impossible for them to smell the presence of the three malicious mogs.

'Why didn't you come to the Pawesome Palace with me?' asked Bobine.

'I thought it would make things worse!'

Bobine nodded forlornly.

'But now . . .' mewed Wolfgang quietly, 'what am I going to do?'

Mulot was feeling so angry his fur had started to stand on end (and there wasn't a cucumber in sight!).

'You're not going to do anything,' he cried. 'But we . . . Why, we're going to grab those chicken-livered cats and—'

'Mulot!' said Bobine sternly. 'No violence, purr-lease! You're too strong, you'd hurt them.'

'Hmmm. I am strong, aren't I?' said Mulot, flexing a muscle.

'Wolfgang,' Couscousse started, 'why didn't you tell us what was going on? We would have helped you.'

'I know. I was just too scared.'

'Well, put that behind you now,' said Couscousse, sweetly. 'There's good news! Berty's
had an idea!'

And she leant towards her friends to whis-
purr her plan.

9. MEOWSTERY UNRAVELLED . . .

That night, for the first time since his arrival at Charamba, Wolfgang slept like a kitten. And understandably so: Mulot had become his bodyguard – he had even set his bed in the corner of Room 13, promising not to move so much as a paw.

The next morning, after Magda's usual rounds, Speed and Hermann went to leave their room for a walk and their daily session of Wolfgang biffing, but found their cat flap blocked.

'Wha—?' They pushed and pushed – with their heads and their paws – but it wouldn't budge.

You see, once Magda had finished clearing the litter trays the night before, Carpette and Couscousse had spent the night gathering books to pile in front of the flap. They'd made a big book tower as high as a perchy pole, to make sure the brothers stayed inside good and propurr!

Then Bobine had done exactly the same to Grievous's cat flap.

All three cats were trapped.

And none of them knew why!

As for Wolfgang, when he stepped into the Pawesome Palace for the first time the next morning, he couldn't believe his eyes! 'Meowzers!' There were boxes and ladders and ropes, and tall windows that showed the trees outside, and scratchy posts and perches and secret passages and tubes, and (Couscousse had been right) loads of cool rectangular thingies everywhere.

Old Prune was sitting on a bright-yellow armchair that made her golden eyes and white fur sparkle in the sunlight. She hissed at him.

Esmeralda was chasing a squidgy ball. She had long, auburn fur, like a lioness's mane. She hissed at him too.

But for the first time since arriving at the hotel, Wolfgang didn't let himself get rattled!

Instead, when Esmeralda curled up to watch him, he walked straight over to fetch the squidgy ball.

Then he and Mulot played like wildcats . . .

'Thanks, Mulot!' Wolfgang panted when they got back to Room 13. 'That was the best fun ever!'

'My purr-leasure! You're one fast cat!'

The next day, Bobine cleared Speed and Hermann's cat flap (just before Magda began her morning rounds) and stepped into their room.

'Well, you took your time!' they complained. 'We've been stuck in here. What's going on?'

'Tsss, tsss, tsss . . .' she hissed sternly. 'Purr-lease don't be rude! Sit down and listen.'

Speed and Hermann weren't brave, so they did as they were told.

'We know exactly what you've been doing,' she started. 'It's not OK to bully other cats.'

'Who? Us? Never!'

I won't go into what Bobine said next (though it was very long and very convincing); let's just say that she knew they were lying and didn't accept any of their rubbish excuses.

'I shut you in here to give you a taste of your own medicine,' she told them. 'So now you have a choice: either you apologize to Wolfgang and leave him in peace for the rest of the holiday, or you stay in your room. If not, I'll let Mulot take care of you, but I wouldn't recommend that option!'

Next Bobine visited Grievous and told him the same thing.

And so later that morning, who should saunter into the Pawesome Palace (under the watchful eye of Mulot), but Grievous, Speed and Hermann, ears flat, on their way to apologize to Wolfgang and promise never to do anything like it ever again.

'Sorry!' they meowed in chorus.

To which Wolfgang could have replied with a whole lot of nasty words, but he didn't. He didn't even scowl. He just said, 'Apology accepted!' then turned around and padded slowly towards Esmeralda.

And this time she didn't hiss or spit.

As he lay down next to her, she just stared at him with her big green eyes. So, Wolfgang dared to stretch out a front leg and tap a squidgy ball towards her paw.

And to his delight, she caught it!

Perched high on her shelf, Bobine watched on with a joyful purr, licking her front paws with great catisfaction.

Siegfried and Constance were doing yoga. Old Prune was dozing in the yellow armchair.

But above all else, Wolfgang was happy again!

They'd done it!

Bobine and her friends had unravelled the meowstery. And now all was well.

Hotel Charamba was saved!

Which meant there was only one thing left to do. The old cat sighed and settled down comfortably. She closed her eyes and purred, 'The right-hand needle goes through the loop, then back on itself . . . Then the loop goes under it . . . No, wait a meowment . . . Over it? Oh no, meowzers. I'm lost!'

And then she fell asleep.

THE END

MARIE PAVLENKO & MARIE VOYELLE

Marie and Marie have known each other for a very long time (their first ever cats were brother and sister, in fact!). Their previous work together includes a graphic novel about ca ... er, no ... walruses!

If Marie Voyelle were a cat, she'd never miss a mealtime. And she'd try to digest her food while lying on Marie Pavlenko's keyboard (preferably while she's working).

If Marie Pavlenko were a cat, she'd spend hours padding through tall grasses, imagining she was in the savannah. And she'd eat dandelions rather than mice.

Marie Voyelle likes drawing animals, people and cars. Sorry, no ... anything BUT cars. They're too hard to draw.

Marie Pavlenko likes writing stories about strong women, elderly couples, runaway spiders and vengeful poos. Oh, and rugged mountains.

ACKNOWLEDGEMENTS

MARIE PAVLENKO

Thank you to everybody in the marvellous Flamm team (Céline, Céline, Céline, yep all three of you, and David, Marine, Shanaz, Eric, Diane, Murielle, Magali and Léa).

Thank you to my fantabulous agents, Roxane Edouard and Claire Nozières for your never-ending support.

Thank you to Marie Voyelle for joining me in this a-meow-zing adventure.

Thank you to my cats Sookie and Obiwan for being such faithful friends.

Thank you to Mathias and Aurélien for adopting Bobine, Carpette, Mulot and Couscousse.

MARIE VOYELLE

I would like to thank Marie for offering me this project. The book makes me laugh every time I read it. Marie, I can safely say, Bobine and her friends are now my friends, thanks to you.

Thank you, too, to everyone at Flammarion for your unfaltering enthusiasm!

And to Saskia, for looking so cute in your cat costume!

And to Kida (my grumpy dragon) and her dragon keepers, Amandine and her family (thank you for helping her thrive as an outdoor cat).

Many thanks also to Gauthier B and your fabulous cat hotel, ARISTIDE.

And finally, to François, and my family and my in-laws (and all your hairy companions ... of the meowing variety, of course). You're all pawsome!

MONSTER BOGEY by ANNA BROOKE
Illustrated by OWEN LINDSAY

Dear nose-pickers, are you well? Good. Then come closer. For I'm about to tell you a right slimer of a tale. In it, there's a bogey monster, two best friends, four daredevil slugs, a neighbour so wicked she'll give you the willy-willy-woo-woos and a castle with secret chambers. Will it end happily? No . . . Yes . . . Sorry, I don't know! You'd better ask the cabaret-singing spider . . .

Paperback, ISBN 978-1-913696-58-0, £7.99 • ebook, ISBN 978-1-913696-81-8, £7.99

PANDA AT THE DOOR by SARAH HORNE

Pudding the panda makes everyone smile at Edinburgh Zoo. But what would make *her* truly happy is a family to take care of – like her heroine, Mary Poppins.

Meanwhile, Callum is having a hard time at home. His parents keep arguing. His sister is annoying, and his ninth birthday gift is a certificate for an 'adopted' panda when all he wanted was Lego.

Then, by a twist of fate, the unbelievable happens and the two come together on Callum's front doorstep . . . Pandamonium!

Paperback, ISBN 978-1-911490-01-2, £6.99 • ebook, ISBN 978-1-913322-23-6, £6.99

MILTON THE MIGHTY by EMMA READ
Illustrated by ALEX G GRIFFITHS

When spider Milton discovers he's been branded deadly, he fears for his life and his species.

Alongside his buddies, big hairy Ralph and daddy-long-legs Audrey, he decides to clear his name. But to succeed, Milton must befriend his house human, Zoe. Is Milton mighty enough to achieve the impossible?

'. . . a charming and thoughtful read.'
THE SCOTSMAN

Paperback, ISBN 978-1-911490-81-4, £6.99 • ebook, ISBN 978-1-912626-31-1, £6.99

THE GREAT CHOCOPLOT by CHRIS CALLAGHAN

It's the end of chocolate – for good! A chocolate mystery . . . At least that's what they're saying on TV.

Jelly and her gran are gobsmacked – they love a Blocka Choca bar or two.

But then a trail of clues leads back to a posh chocolate shop in town owned by the distinctly bitter Garibaldi Chocolati.

Is it really the chocopocalypse, or a chocoplot to be cracked?

With an excellent cast of characters, laugh-out-loud moments, and witty and sharp observations, this is a great choice for fans of Dahl and Walliams.
GUARDIAN

Paperback, ISBN 978-1-910002-51-3, £6.99 • ebook, ISBN 978 -1-910655-57-3, £6.99